Fortnite Tale: A Changing World

Book #2 in Series

by

Author Art

Paperback Editic

D1468556

TABLE OF CONTENTS

A Word From Author Art

A Word From Author Art

Hey everyone! Author Art here! This book took a while to make, but that's because it's twice the length of the first book. So much more action, adventure, and humor in this book than the last one! Oh, and more characters! That's always great!

For me to keep making these books, **I need your help!** Leaving me a **five-star review** helps me in the same way subscribing to your favorite Youtuber does.

I comment on all my reviews so make sure to check yours a day after its posted =)

Have a parent leave a review for you if you cannot.

Also, make sure to **follow me on Amazon** to be notified when my next book is released. My blog is also posted there, on my Amazon Author Page – giving you the latest news about what I'm doing. Other social media links will be provided near the end of this book.

I sincerely hope you enjoy this installment of Fortnite Tale!

<u>Chapter 1:</u> First, You Train

"You sure about this?" questioned John, who looked at Fate with angst.

"Nah, you might get erased from existence." replied Fate, acting out of character.

"Oh." a surprised John said. "That's cool."

"Seriously though, this is a waste of time, shouldn't I go find, what's her name, the Bite Bumber?"

"Haha." Fate chuckled.

"Bite Bumber? It's Brite Bomber, John."

"Yeah whatever why are we arguing semantics?" exclaimed John.

"I don't think you used that word correctly, you see — "

John interrupted Fate and said,

"You're like, supposed to be this powerful wizard and you keep fooling around. Let's just start the training now, even though I think it's a waste of time."

John. It's just a façade. Ever since Omen died, I've been trying to act joyful, and wittier. Like you. But the pain is still there. Fate thought to herself.

"It's not a waste of time." Fate said.

"Have you noticed that you seem to run into enemies, quite a bit?"

"Yeah." John sighed. "I know."

If I was better prepared when I was with Omen, maybe, just maybe, he would still be here with us... but that kind of thinking is bad too. I can't let it get to me. I'm acting like I don't need training but she's right, I do. It's just I'm so frustrated and want to find Brite Bomber ASAP. I don't want to lose more people. John thought to himself.

"So what kind of training are we going to do?"

Fate replied by saying,

"Well, it all starts off with me tossing you into a volcano. After you get out, you have to escape a giant tarantula that is trying to eat you. Then – and only then – will you be qualified enough to begin the real training: read one hundred of Amazon's Fortnite Guide Books."

No! Not Fortnite Guide Books! Why oh why would someone read those when you can just watch Ninja, Tfue, Dakotaz, Daequan, Nick Eh, Myth and all those beasts on YouTube for free!? John thought.

"Uhh, yeah, cool, alright." John murmured.

"So... how is all that gonna help me exactly?"

"I'm just rustling your jimmies John." a playful Fate said, giving John a light smile.

Rustle... my jimmies? That's an old meme Fate, get with the times. It was never dank to begin with.

The Gorilla was cute though. John thought to himself.

"Okay…" John said.

"So, the real training, what's it going to be lady?"

"I'm going to run a training simulation for you." Fate said.

"You will be dropped into a private Fortnite server, and face some of my illusions. If you get hit once, you lose and the simulation resets."

"But aren't you very weak though?" John said,

with a tone of worry.

Fate replied by saying,

"Weaker than I was in my prime, yes. But, I can

still do many things. It's just that the scale at

which I can do things has gone down. These

illusions, they're much weaker than the ones I

used to be able to cast. And they don't last as long."

"A few things first. You've seen enemies build, but

you've never actually built yourself. In the Fortnite

Servers, kids use things called controllers,

typically, to build structures within the game. In

the Fortnite Source, however, it is willpower

based."

"Willpower based?" said John.

"Like a green lantern ring?"

Fate replied,

"I don't know what that is John, due to potential

copyright infringement. I'm going to pretend you

didn't say that."

Fate are you just going to keep on breaking the

fourth wall for the rest of my journey? John

thought.

"It's going to feel very weird, the ability to create by just thinking about it. Although, it isn't exactly out of thin air. When you build, a blueprint will appear in your hand and you will have to draw what you are going to build."

Well, now I feel bad about not taking those drawing classes in high school. John thought.

"I suck at drawing though." lamented John.

"It doesn't matter." Fate replied.

"It's just basic lines and shapes that you're going to have to draw."

"Yeah I don't think I can do that Fate." said John.

"Lines... shapes... it might as well be Da Vinci."

"Da Vinci? The Tom Hanks movie?" Fate asked.

There she goes... again. John thought to himself.

"Umm, no." said John.

"The painter, from way back in the day. Did a lot of things back then. Come to think of it, the dude was probably an alien."

"Oh, I see." Fate said.

"Well, we should begin now. This first simulation, you won't be armed. It is to prepare you to defend yourself only. Just try to build walls to protect yourself, John."

"Alrighty." said John. "Let's do this!"

Ten failed simulations later.

"Let's not do this anymore, Fate."

How the simulations went down:

<u>Simulation 1:</u>

John panicked and ran away from an enemy. He got shot in the back.

<u>Simulation 2:</u>

John panicked and ran away from an enemy. He got shot in the back.

<u>Simulation 3:</u>

John panicked and ran away from an enemy. No – he didn't get shot in the back this time. He ran too far and fell off a cliff.

Simulation 4:

John tried building a wall but drew a circle instead of a square. He really is a terrible drawer! And then he got shot. From the front.

Simulation 5:

John was furious and tried to Kung-Fu kick the enemy. He got shot. From the front.

Simulation 6:

John was furious and tried his best Conor Mcregor on the enemy. He got shot. From the front.

Simulation 7:

John tried his best Professor X impression and tried thinking really hard about building a wall.

Success! He built his first wall. Well, he actually built a rooftop instead. (Every new player ever lol.) Then he got shot. From the front.

Simulation 8:

John built a wall successfully! But then he got shot. From all angles. Building one wall is not good enough John!

Simulation 9:

This is too embarrassing for the narrator to discuss. John, what were you thinking?

Simulation 10:

Throwing apples and mushrooms does not damage anyone, John. Lmao.

"I mean, you didn't do so bad, John." Fate consoled.

"To be honest, I thought you wouldn't be able to build anything. It's a difficult skill to master."

"Yeah, no kidding." said John.

"First time I saw the blueprint in my hands, it was a weird feeling. And then I messed up my drawing and got shot. Don't you have any tips for me?"

Fate thought for a moment and told John,

"Let's see… Well, I was going to tell you to just pretend like you're an architect, but I think that's too complicated for you,"

John interjected,

"Too complicated for me? What are you trying to say, Fate?"

"maybe you should try to do – " Fate was interrupted by Leviathan.

Did you feel that? Leviathan said.

Feel what? Fate said, confused.

Someone has crossed over to the real world.

Leviathan said.

John, is he finished with his training?

No. Fate said. *He can barely build a wall.*

"Fate, try to do what?" asked John. "You there?"

"I'm sorry John." said Fate. "Just hold up."

This is not good. Leviathan said.

John is nowhere near close enough to unlocking his love wings. And we're too weak at the moment to create a rift for him to travel. Then that means, the only way to contact Brite Bomber is to meet her in a Fortnite Server match.

But how will we find her that way? a worried Fate asked.

Dozens of thousands of matches are run at the same time. More than that, even. There's no way we'll be able to detect the one she is in, not with our current power.

I might be able to pull from my life energy to fuel my telepathic abilities. Leviathan said.

No! Fate exclaimed.

You're already so weak – you can't afford to do that. Let me do it instead...

I'm sorry Fate, but you are the future. Leviathan said.

You, John, and Brite Bomber. Maybe others. My time is limited, I will do this for the future.

I – I hate that you have to do this. Fate lamented.

But I understand. I hate it, but I understand. How much of your life energy will be taken?

Enough life will be left that I can still help you and John on the journey ahead, I assure you of that.

Leviathan said.

I see. Fate sighed.

Continue training John, as much as you can.

Leviathan commanded.

When I have narrow down the location of Brite Bomber, I will contact you again.

I understand. Fate declared.

Sad at the fact that Leviathan was going to have to cut his life shorter than expected, but understanding the purpose of it all, Fate continued to train John and gave it her all.

During John's training, he gained a foundational knowledge of battle. He learned about each weapon, including their strengths, weaknesses, and best situations to use them in. He learned about building, including the most common structures used in battle, and when to use certain

structures.

Finally, he learned about items: their uses and

when to use them.

However, the foundational knowledge that he was

given was no supplement to authentic experience,

which he would later find out.

Fate looked towards John and asked, "How do you

feel, John?"

"Like doodoo." John joked, eyes squinting.

"Nah, but seriously, that's how I'm supposed to feel like, two days after training. It's a good thing."

"What do you mean, John?" a confused Fate asked.

John began to stretch his arms and said,

"Training was tough, and I learned a lot."

Fate looked at John in amusement and replied,

"You thought that was tough?"

"We did VERY basic training, John."

John stopped stretching and looked Fate directly in the eye, saying,

"Basic to you, but not to me. I'm still a beginner, and it was tough for me."

Sometimes his more serious side comes out and he makes total sense. Fate thought to herself.

"You're right, sorry to belittle you." Fate apologized.

John and Fate got one day of rest before Fate was contacted by Leviathan, informing her that the location of Brite Bomber was located.

With absolute certainty, Leviathan knew that Brite Bomber was in a duos game but could not narrow down her location to one specific match.

Two potential matches were identified as holding Brite Bomber.

"Why don't you and I split up, Fate?" John said.

"It is a reasonable plan, barring the fact that you are inexperienced." Fate declared.

"So, no."

Leviathan contacted Fate and told her to let John

on his own. It would serve as valuable experience,

he said. Fate did not like the idea, but trusted

Leviathan's wisdom, and gave John the permission

to go alone. Their matches would both go wildly

different.

Chapter 2: Then, You Play

Fate's Match

So… Earth's Fortnite is in late Season 2 now. Brite Bomber must surely be a force to be reckoned with now. If there is one certainty about this match, it is that she will show up in the top ten players, bare minimum. She should not be difficult to locate, if in fact she is in this match.

Fate disguised herself as a default skin and dropped off in Lonely Lodge.

It is always so strange, playing a virtual recreation of Lonely Lodge. It makes you wonder what is really real in the universe.

Fate landed at Lonely partly for the strange vibe she got from landing in the recreation of a place she grew up in, and partly for strategic reasons.

She landed in the watchtower and spotted a pair of players landing in the large cabin close to her.

I wonder if they spotted me. I am desperately trying to go unavoided. In any case, I need to come down from here and search for weapons.

Alright I've searched all the chests that were here. They didn't all spawn this time, unfortunately. Green AR will have to do for now. Did not get any shield, I'll have to be careful.

Fate came down from the watch tower and began to farm some wood.

At the seventy-wood point, she stopped abruptly. From the corner of her eye, she could see a stray player that was aiming directly at her.

I didn't see this player!

Fate got shot at, but not before she could build a stair-wall combo to protect herself.

Fate was getting shot at by a semi-automatic sniper, which was not very effective against her wall. Still, Fate was cautious.

Now, I need to build around me, and make myself a one-by-one. There. The pair that dropped in front of me will probably make an appearance soon. Now, time to fire back!

Fate began to fire back at the enemy, who was another default skin. The enemy had no building materials and was quickly mowed down.

It is done. From here, it looks like he did not drop much.

Fate decided that it was not worth leaving her one-by-one tower to pick up the semi-auto sniper that the player dropped, along with some bandages.

I'll just wait here until that pair of players comes out. It will be two versus one, but I have got a great position.

She waited, and waited, but they did not come. The storm began to close in, and she decided to head out.

Storm is coming in quick, but I do not think that it will touch me.

She began to go in the direction of Retail Row,

which was inside the circle. As she approached the

side of Retail Row with the buildings in between

the transmission and water tower, she spotted two

wooden three-by-three towers, on the taller

buildings in the middle. Each tower was opposite

the other one, each occupying one building.

Oh no, it must be the pair from before! I'll have to –

GETS SHOT AT FROM HER RIGHT SIDE

What!?

Immediately after getting hit, Fate enclosed

herself in a one-by-one tower, with a roof on top of

the top wall, and stairs in front of her side wall, for extra security.

Using the then-allowed trick to see through the walls by editing, she saw that she was getting rushed by two players from her right. But, at the same time, the people in the towers revealed themselves, and began to fire at Fate.

Why are the two in front of me firing at me when they can shoot these other two out in the open?

Fate kept replacing the walls that were getting destroyed and was quickly starting to run out of resources.

There's only two ways that I can go now... to my left, and to my behind. If I go to my left, I can still get shot at from the people in front of me. If I go from behind...

A half-second before running out of mats, Fate did the seemingly illogical and escaped from behind, running towards the storm. She was out of line of sight while doing so.

The storm is not doing that much damage at the moment. I can stay here for a little while. I have enough bandages to heal myself back to seventy-five health.

Fate's plan was to stay inside the storm, behind a tree, while the pair from lonely lodge and the pair in the towers, would eliminate each other.

Then, she would wait until the very last second possible to escape the storm, hoping that the winning pair would give up on Fate, determining that she was already dead.

Okay, I have to wait until the right moment. Just a little longer. Now, time to go.

Fate waited until the exact, perfect moment, and escaped the storm. Checking in every direction, she could not spot any players as she went on ahead.

As the match progressed, the number of people alive began to dwindle, in the typical fashion, but something... odd began to happen.

34 Players remaining

31 Players remaining

28 Players remaining

31 Players remaining

Wait, what? The numbers went back to 31?

38 Players remaining

44 Players remaining

47 Players remaining

Why is the number of players increasing? And why is it increasing so fast?

Each second, the number of players left kept increasing in a random increment. Fate was startled.

This is unusual... why –

A mysterious voice called out.

"Fate, come with me!"

John's Match

Got the noob that was in this building with me. Anarchy Acres, not exactly a friendly sounding name. Hopefully, not much anarchy goes on this match. I think there were only two other people that landed here besides the noob I just killed. I probably shouldn't be calling him a noob on the account of this is the first Fortnite match I'm playing.

John searched the whole house, having great luck at his side.

Ooh, this is the SCAR that Fate mentioned. She said that it was the best overall gun. Nice!

Got a bunch of extras too. Shield, med kits, some grenades. I'm stacked!

While John was doing the default dance in his joy at getting lucky with his first chests, the teammate of the killed noob started breaking in from the top of the house.

OH CRA - I MEAN, CRUD! I totally forgot that this is duos. I probably made too much noise dancing too. Well, I'd better kill him before he gets me.

John went up the stairs and was ready to shoot at the player once he broke in but stopped.

The player did not switch to his weapon, and instead began talking to John.

"Are you hacking?" the player said.

John scratched his head and replied, "Umm, no?"

The player began to examine John and asked, "How did you get that awesome outfit?"

John looked at himself and realized why the player began to ask him that question.

Dang it Fate, weren't you supposed to make me blend in? Now Ali-A is going to make a video about a "leaked" skin of some guy in a black suit with a beard.

"Oh, what the heck?" John tried to act confused.

"I – I dunno. Maybe a glitch or something."

The player moved in closer to John and told him,

"Hey stay there, lemme take a screenshot."

John realized something and looked at the player, asking,

"Hey, aren't you mad that I killed your friend though?"

"Huh?" the player responded, in complete confusion.

"... the guy with the blonde hair?" John replied.

"One of the default skins?" the player said.

"I'm playing solo duos though."

That means...

The front of the house was blown up as John

realized that the teammate of the player he killed

was still out there.

"We need to team up!" John yelled.

The player looked at John and replied "Okay!"

"Let's break through this wall!"

John and the player proceeded to break through

the wall of the room they were in and went outside.

Once outside, the player built a wall in front of

them. He and John began to wait for the enemy.

"You see anyone to your side?" John asked.

"No, you?" the player responded.

"I think I can hear him coming. Let me – "

As the player began to peak his head out to look, he immediately got shot twice. An accurate two-burst with the burst assault rifle took him down. John never got the chance to ask the poor soul for his name.

No! He was a nice guy. It's not like he actually died in real life or anything, but still.

Without any warning, the player began to build a large structure on top of the house. It was a four-by-four structure.

How is he building so quick like that? He's a default, is that Tfue? This is bad. I can run back towards the house, but that'll leave me exposed for a few seconds. He's a good shot.

John was in a terrible situation. He had the positional disadvantage, along with not having the suitable weaponry for the situation. With no resources, he could not go on the offensive by rushing the player either. In all sense of the word, he was trapped.

I can't die like this. I need to find Brite Bomber!

Hey, what the heck is that guy doing? Tossing up

LOL emoticons, and riding the pony? He thinks he's

so good...

"Hey, you in the tower!" an unknown girl shouted.

"Are you bullying a player?"

"Yeah, so?" the player said, full of himself.

"He's a noob, I can do whatever I want to him."

"Is that so?" the unknown girl replied.

"Three... two... one..."

SPLAT

The whole house came crashing down, which brought the tower down with it. Fortunately, the cocky player inside did not survive. Good riddance!

"Back to the lobby for that guy!" the unknown girl shouted.

"Hey, you can come out now, I won't hurt you."

How did this girl even know what was going on?

"Yeah, alright." John said. "Hey... it's you..."

Brite Bomber's facial expression and tone

completely changed when she saw John. With a

mixture of rage and fear, she yelled,

"Why do you keep following me, go away!"

Why do I keep following her? What?

John looked directly into Brite Bomber's eyes, held

his hands out, and tried to calm her down.

"Look – I'm not who you think I am."

"My name is John, and I'm the good guy."

"The first time I would have agreed with you."

Brite Bomber said, a little calmer than before.

"But what you did – tried to do to me the second

time… you're a monster! Why would I ever help

you?"

John softened his tone and said,

"Look, I'm just going to go ahead and say it."

"You're going to think I'm crazy. I would think that

if I was told this, too. But there's a guy that looks

just like me. He's The Reaper. He is the one who

spoke to you."

"I'm John, John Wick. Like from the Keanu Reeves movie. This is gonna sound even crazier but a powerful being sent me to find you, because you have a special ability. And you're going to help us save the world."

"Oh... no wonder you always looked so familiar." Brite Bomber said.

"Good movie."

"You're right. All of what you said is... totally crazy. I don't really believe you, but I want to. Just because I want to learn more about this special ability I supposedly have. And a powerful being? I want to know more. Still, prove to me why you're

the good guy, cause this is too much."

Okay, how can I prove I'm the good guy to her. I

guess I just gotta prove I'm a normal guy. The

Reaper probably always comes off as a psycho when

he talks to Brite Bomber.

"You know Snobby Shores, the actual Snobby

Shores on Earth?" John asked.

"Yeah." Brite Bomber answered.

"I used to want to be rich, so I would go there and try to learn how to invest in real estate from the snobs there. And it didn't go well. And then one of the guy's daughters threw like a massive beach ball at me. And I started to… cry."

Brite Bomber was trying to contain her laughter, and with a slight smirk replied, "Oh, yeah?"

John pointed at Brite Bomber and shouted, "Hey, I can see you're laughing!"

Brite Bomber could not contain her laughter any longer.

"Hahaha. It's cause you mentioned it. I wasn't gonna laugh, I swear. You pointed it out!"

"Do you believe me now, though?" John asked.

"I mean, I guess." Brite bomber declared. "But..."

"When I was first contacted by the guy that looks like you... he told me his name was John Wick. And to not trust the man without the face? And he showed up recently, again..."

The storm began to close in on them.

"Hey, the storm is coming. I'll tell you what happened on our way out."

The storm began to close in and the circle moved towards Loot Lake.

As Brite Bomber and John Wick spoke on their way towards Loot Lake, several revelations were made.

"You just took care of those two guys on our way here like it was nothing!" John said in excitement.

Glad she's gonna be on our side.

"I play this game too much." Brite Bomber responded.

"I can't believe all those things you said though." John said.

"What he said to you... how he would put your friends and family in Fortnite... and make you kill them over and over again and make them suffer that. The Reaper... he's a demon."

"And what he said about a hunt for the Hidden Keys going on. People are getting killed in the real world to find information about them. It's unreal..."

As John was talking, Brite Bomber kept shifting her eyes from looking to the floor to looking at John. Each time she looked at John, she had a look on her, as if she wanted to tell him something. But something kept preventing her from doing so.

Leviathan called out to John,

John, I'm going to teleport you back to Lonely Lodge. This is urgent. If you have found Brite Bomber, hold on to her.

Chapter 3: Leviathan's True Nature

John and Brite Bomber were transported to Lonely Lodge, where Leviathan would have several important messages to give.

Leviathan began to monologue,

"I must get all this information out at once. The most pressing matter is Fate is gone. I do not know where she is. I am too weak to locate her. Initially, I thought it was the presence that I sensed who crossed over to the real world that might have crossed back to the Fortnite Servers to get Fate. But I do not think this is the case. It appears that another entity is responsible for taking Fate. I can only hope it is an ally in incognito. And there is

more, so much more."

"I can sense subtle movements in the earth of the

Fortnite Source. It may sound trivial, but to create

even the slightest of movements that can be

detected from this location requires a great force.

This force can cause changes in the Fortnite

Servers... the extent of which, I do not know."

"And perhaps the most haunting, is of a dream I

had. A day dream. A man with an animal skull for

a mask. A werewolf. And others which my memory

has blurred out. This... is an omen."

"I also saw new allies rising to help our cause…

but at the rate in which our allies rose was

disproportionately smaller than the rate in which

they fell… "

After Leviathan was finished prophesizing, John

and Brite Bomber updated him with news of The

Reaper and the Hidden Keys. Leviathan was

shocked at the existence of the Hidden Keys and

could not figure out their purpose.

Brite Bomber mentioned that The Reaper said it

would open a bridge between humans and deities,

but Leviathan thought that notion was absurd.

Leviathan told them that only those with Love Wings can act as a natural liaison between the world of the humans and beyond. And those who have Love Wings are rare individuals that are both pure and fallen.

Confused, Leviathan only knew of one person that could help him find answers. But it was going to be a risky journey.

"You two have to stay here." Leviathan commanded.

"I'm going to visit a man I once called my best friend."

FLASHBACK TO LEVIATHAN'S YOUTH

Two children are playing in a large open field. The game is to roll down the hill as quickly as you can. Whoever loses has to eat one of the many rotten apples that are lying around.

"It's no fair! You won because you have that fishbowl!" a young boy shouted.

"That helps you roll down faster!"

"I'm just better at this game than you are, that's all." a young Leviathan said.

The young boy, discouraged, looked at Leviathan and said,

"But you beat me at everything..."

"No, you can predict stuff way better than I can." young Leviathan replied.

"A few years ago, you said that around this time there was going to be a period where I won all our games, and you were right!"

"Well I don't remember that." the young boy said.

"I guess that's one thing you're better than me at too, memory."

"Come on, we can do something else." young Leviathan said.

"Hey, I know what we can do. Let's climb the watchtower!"

"But that's dangerous!" the young boy exclaimed.

"That's what makes it fun!" Leviathan replied.

The young boy agreed, with must resistance, to climb the watchtower with Leviathan. Up they went, with Leviathan climbing it at a much faster rate than his friend.

As they climbed the watchtower, Leviathan's friend started to look down, and grew with fear.

He started to shake and lose his grip. Leviathan noticed, and tried to come down to help his friend, but it was too late. His friend fell from the watchtower and broke his back.

An already strong friendship grew more after this event. Leviathan spent months caring for his friend, nursing him back to health, and helped ease his fear of heights too.

"You know, I'm afraid of heights because of my sister..." the young boy said.

"She would always tell me that I could never reach great heights, that's the word she always used. She said I could never fly as high as she could."

"It just hurt me so much because it was my sister telling me that. That's why I flew to this world, your world. I don't know how I got here exactly but I'm glad I did."

"I guess it's just in our blood as Ravens to fly to where we feel the safest. Leviathan, I feel safe with you, you're like my brother, my real brother. And I'm never going to leave you."

FLASHBACK ENDS

Leviathan has arrived at a small cabin. There, he phases down through the floor, and enters a large, dark room, where a man is waiting for him.

"How many millions of years has it been since you last visited me?" the mysterious man said.

"You know how many, and you know why I have not visited you in this long, Raven. The man without a face is what you're being called now."

The Raven replied with, "Suppose it does fit my appearance."

"You know why I am here, Raven." Leviathan said.

"Of course, I do." The Raven said. "But first..."

The whole area began to submerge in darkness; The Raven began to toy with Leviathan.

"Let's see the once great Leviathan in action!"

Phantom human enemies and monsters began to swarm Leviathan from all directions.

Leviathan just stood there. In the exact moment that the enemies were a split second from touching him, in one swift move, perhaps in a single millisecond, Leviathan pulled out a colorful pickaxe, glowing blue, purple, green, and pink, and struck them all down. They disappeared.

"I'm impressed." The Raven began to clap.

"Bravo! With speed and ability like that, you surely could take on all your enemies single-handedly."

Leviathan rebuked him by stating,

"You know why I can't do that, Raven."

The Raven mocked Leviathan,

"Oh, because you're afraid your true nature will come out? You're afraid that you're going to feast on the energy and emotions of the things in your world that are keeping you from your loneliness?"

"You play the part of a wise sage..."

"But you are the definition of a wolf in sheep's clothing. You are the reason for why this world is the way it is, why it became violent, and why it's starting to change. Your kind is a cosmic virus that just destroys."

"All those spirits that left you and went to Wailing Woods, one of them being The Black Knight – what do you think they have been doing? Celebrating the fact that half of their population was consumed – by you? The person that they thought loved them?"

"Stop it." Leviathan commanded.

"It was in the past, and it was an action I did not willingly commit."

The Raven replied,

"Conveniently, it was not you that mass murdered thousands of spirits. Spirits that were on their way to grow up. Grow up and be powerful, too much for you to control. Factions have risen, Leviathan, and they're all coming after you. A part of your inner evil has rubbed off on them and they're not going after just revenge. They're going to go after humans too. They want you to feel the pain they felt when they woke up to their friends and family members being eradicated from existence."

Leviathan began to become furious.

"Are you mad, Leviathan? Do you want to consume me too?" The Raven mocked.

"Have you told John and Fate yet, about Omen? About how you sent Omen to get Fate, despite knowing that he was likely not going to survive that day? Out of fear that he was going to leave, with Fate, you killed him. It was you that killed him, no one else. You creatures are leeches. In your loneliness, you do everything you can to get rid of that feeling, and that includes using people to your advantage."

"It took you hundreds of thousands of years to ever mention the war between the Ravens and the

Leviathans. How our kind hates each other. The moment you told me about that, I knew you had been using me for all that time. That's why I set as many spirits as I could have free, that day."

"The Ravens manipulated you to want to come to this world so that I would consume you. I did not." Leviathan stated.

"No, you did not. But you should have. I'll let you know about the Hidden Keys. Just so you can have the illusion of hope. Just like how the spirits had an illusion, of friendship." The Raven said.

"There are many different Hidden Keys, each with distinct properties. They began to develop that fateful day you decided to massacre so many spirits. Even the Fortnite Source knew that you were a threat that needed to be exterminated. They aren't actual keys. They're the real, sacred versions of the pickaxes found in the Fortnite Servers."

"There is one that you should be worried about right now, Leviathan. It is a key that was specifically created just to kill you."

Leviathan felt a great pain in his chest when The Raven told him that there were items that the world created just to kill him.

The Raven noted Leviathan's pain and began to mock Leviathan again,

"Ironic, isn't it? That the world you created, created something of its own? For the sole purpose of killing you."

"It is a pickaxe that looks like the standard one, but the difference is that this one is very durable, very heavy, and very powerful. You will know when you see it, with its rust and chains. It is meant to break your helmet and deprive you of that special water you need to survive."

"Leviathan, one last thing. The Reaper. You may think that I created The Reaper. But, as much as I wish that were true, it simply isn't. The Reaper is the darkest creation of this world. The Reaper is pure chaos and dark mischief. Why it looks just like John, who knows. I have my own Reaper's Bane, but if at all possible, get rid of that nuisance for me, will you?"

"Thank you for the knowledge, Raven." Leviathan said.

"I am sorry that things could not go the way they were supposed to."

The Raven replied,

"Oh Leviathan, things never go the way they are supposed to go, never."

"Where is Fate?" Leviathan asked.

"Back at Lonely Lodge." The Raven replied.

<u>Chapter 4:</u> Battles In and Out

Two whole months had passed since Brite Bomber was recruited by John, and Leviathan met with the Raven. It was now Season 3 in the Fortnite Servers.

In those two months, Fate managed to heal fully, but she was never going to be as powerful as she once was. Leviathan warned Fate that she was on her last life, and if anything were to happen to her, she would disappear from the Fortnite Source forever.

With her strength back, Fate committed to training John, while Brite Bomber trained on her own, who was much more advanced than John.

Fate kept to herself what happened to her the day she and John went looking for Brite Bomber. Leviathan was just glad that she was back, and in full health.

While Leviathan and his team underwent training, an important battle took place at Wailing Woods between The Black Knight and The Reaper.

"Tell me where you took her!" screamed The Black Knight.

The Reaper glared at The Black Knight, amused at the anger he was giving off.

The Black Knight began to fire at The Reaper with his modified revolver, a guaranteed one-hit kill weapon.

But The Reaper kept on building, and building, and building, and building... It appeared that The Reaper could pull from an infinite number of resources.

This is terrible ... I don't have the required firepower to go through his walls... I don't think he can even run out of resources... Blasted Reaper!

"Blue Squire, Royale Knight, go!" The Black Knight commanded.

The Blue Squire and Royale Knight, The Black Knight's closest confidants, began to flank The Reaper at his command. They used the stairs-wall combo to gain three stories of height on him, and then proceeded to build floors towards his location.

The Reaper now had to worry about The Black Knight directly in front of him, while The Blue Squire attacked from his left, and Royale Knight attacked from his right, all from higher ground.

As he was being rushed, The Reaper pulled out double hand cannons, and headshotted both The Blue Squire, and The Royale Knight. Immediately, they went down.

"No!" shouted The Black Knight. "No!"

The Black Knight began to build a bridge towards The Reaper as fast as he could and dropped from above to land directly next to The Reaper, who was inside a two-by-two wooden tower.

Not having his gun reloaded, he pulled out his pickaxe, Axecalibur and swung at The Reaper's head, but The Reaper dodged the would-be fatal blow.

"YOU DEMON!" The Black Knight shouted, with pure anger.

The Black Knight kept swinging Axecalibur at The Reaper, but each time, The Reaper swiftly dodged each blow.

What? Not even a graze? Impossible!

The Black Knight continued to swing Axecalibur at The Reaper, with each miss, causing him to grow in frustration. With his anger growing, his swings began to grow wider and heavier.

Is he... phasing through my attacks?

The Reaper began to smirk after each miss.

The Black Knight was now more frustrated than ever, tossing Axecalibur at The Reaper, and pulling out his modified revolver again, to reload it.

Right as The Black Knight was pulling out his revolver, The Reaper made a dash towards

Axecalibur, almost ghost-like, pushed himself against the wooden wall behind him, and smashed The Black Knight on his head, knocking out his helmet.

THUMP!

You could feel the concussive force as the large, heavy axecalibur smashed against the sturdy Black Knight's helmet. The Black Knight only managed to pull out his revolver halfway through in the time it took The Reaper to grab Axecalibur, and then bounce off the wall to attack him.

"Ahh!" The Black Knight screeched, as he was

brought down to the wooden floor.

"I didn't like that scream." The Reaper said. "Let's

try this again."

The Reaper went to pick up The Black Knight's

helmet and put it back on him.

"Round two, here we go."

"AHH!" The Black Knight screeched again, with more agony than the last time.

"I would do a round three..." The Reaper stated.

"... but you're getting too weak to scream loudly. I got something better, though, just wait."

"Here, drink this." The Reaper told The Black Knight, as he force-fed him some Chug Jug.

The Black Knight regained his strength, and immediately tried to punch The Reaper, who dodged the hit.

"No, no, Lucan." The Reaper said. "You stay there."

The Reaper stomped on The Black Knight's face, but not hard enough to make him lose consciousness. He had something important to show him.

"I want to show you that anyone, anyone, can become me." The Reaper claimed.

"Don't care if you're a kid, a woman, there's me in everyone. Come out from behind the trees, darling. It's time!"

The Reaper tossed out The Black Knight from the two-by-two structure as a figure emerged from the trees, wearing a knight's outfit, a red knight's outfit. On the floor, The Black Knight began to tilt his head upwards.

"Looking the wrong way, Lucan." The Reaper said, as he moved his head towards the correct direction. "Take your helmet off, darling."

The Red Knight took off her helmet and revealed herself to be the long-lost wife of Lucan, Mirabelle.

"No..." Lucan murmured. "Mira..."

Before Lucan could say his wife's full name, he was knocked out cold by The Reaper, and was left to suffer.

"If you die, it means you were weak and will not be worth playing with anymore. You'll respawn even weaker and at that point, why would I bother with you?"

"If you live, it means you were strong. You'll come after me with hate, stronger than you were today. And you'll be fun to play with."

"I lose nothing with leaving you here. Darling, you get one of those knights, and I'll take the other. We'll need them for later."

The Red Knight replied,

"Did that man know me once?"

The Reaper exclaimed,

"He knew you, every bit of you, except the most important part of you. He neglected that part and know you're mine."

Back at Lonely Lodge, Brite Bomber and John continued to train under Fate.

Brite Bomber continued to increase her skills at a rapid-pace, while John was slow to improve.

Amongst humans in the Fortnite Servers, Brite Bomber was an elite player, easily amongst the top one percent of one percent of players. John, on the other hand... was more like on the top of one percent... of the worst players in Fortnite.

A sloppy builder, a panicky shooter, with terrible environmental awareness, it is unclear why Leviathan thought John was meant to be the protector of worlds.

Could it be that Leviathan was wrong about John?

The evidence seemed to stack against John being a savior or protector. He never displayed any heroic characteristics prior to being recruited. In fact, his sole purpose in life was to gain riches so he could live an easy life. Were Leviathan's waning powers the reason for his misjudgment of John? Or is there something to John that remains to be seen?

Why am I progressing so slowly? John thought to himself.

This is incredibly frustrating. I've been told that there's children who play this game, back on Earth, who can hang with the elites. Why is it taking so long for me to get better?

Fate sensed that John was frustrated and asked, "John, what's wrong?"

"It's been two months of training and I don't feel like I've gotten any better." John replied.

"I've got the basics down, thank Epic Games, but it's frustrating now. All these advanced building techniques. It's like I need a degree in architecture to learn all this."

"No, John. I did tell you that childr – "

"Yeah, yeah, children learn this stuff quickly and they become elite players." a frustrated John said.

"And that's what's bugging me. I'm more than a decade older than your average eight-year-old and I can't even play at that level. It's demoralizing. I mean, look at Brite Bomber and how she's progressing so quickly, why can she grow like that and not me?"

"Humans are all different like that." Fate said.

"Varying strengths and weaknesses. Leviathan chose you for a reason."

"I'm starting to think he was wrong about me." a demoralized John sighed.

A few days later, Leviathan informed the group that he had located one of the Hidden Keys.

According to Leviathan, it would be somewhere inside or around the prison. He sent John and Brite Bomber to go look for it, which was inside the prison of the Fortnite Source.

Fate was not sent with them because Leviathan needed Fate to stay at Lonely for a special task.

"Alright, we're approaching the prison, be careful."
John told Brite Bomber.

"This place brings back memories, I got my first
dub here." said Brite Bomber.

"Beat a couple of knights."

"Knights? The Black Knight?" John asked.

"How did you know?" Brite Bomber said.

Brite Bomber revealed to John that she beat the
Blue Squire, Royale Knight, and The Black Knight

way back. She told John that they were bullies,

and they needed to be dealt with. John thought it

was unusual that she would have encountered

them, especially considering that The Black

Knight did not seem like the type of person that

would be messing around in the Fortnite Servers.

In any case, John decided that the conversation

would best be continued back at Lonely Lodge, as

they had a mission at hand. They continued to

search the prison and found a familiar face inside

one of the cells.

"Speak of the devil and he shall appear." John

said.

"What is the mighty Lucan doing here?"

Lucan responded,

"Looks like the devil is right behind you."

Confused, John turned around, and was hit in the head by Brite Bomber's pickaxe, Rainbow Smash.

He was then tossed inside the cell with Lucan, and Brite Bomber began to talk to John once he regained consciousness.

"Where does Leviathan keep his spectral axe!?" Brite Bomber shouted.

"What are you doing?" a groggy John asked.

"We aren't your enemy…"

"Clearly, she thinks you are." Lucan interjected.

"If you don't answer, I'll shoot you!" Brite Bomber shouted again.

"John Wick predicted all your lies, he told me everything that you would say when I would first encounter you, Reaper."

"What?" John was confused.

Brite Bomber continued to ramble about the predictions that "John Wick" told her about.

He predicted that "The Reaper" would appear to Brite Bomber in a game of Fortnite, near Anarchy Acres. He then predicted that "The Reaper" would try to convince her that he was good by telling her a story about Snobby Shores. Finally, "John Wick" gave her a story that she could use to tell "The Reaper", making it seem like she was like an innocent victim.

Brite Bomber was convinced that the man she had been with was not the real John Wick, but instead The Reaper. She then revealed that during those two months, she was impressed at how well-hidden

Leviathan's Spectral Axe was, because there was

no sign of it anywhere.

Lucan noticed that there was something off about

the story that she was telling.

"The Reaper can't make predictions." said Lucan.

"He isn't like Leviathan, or Fate, or The Raven.

He's a powerful entity but does not have the power

of foresight. He's simply unrelenting chaos."

"You are being played, Brite Bomber. Listen to your friend, John here."

Brite Bomber began to become conflicted. All this time, she believed The Reaper to be the true, good John Wick. But Lucan made her think about the whole situation. He sounded right.

"But... why?" Brite Bomber asked.

"Psychological warfare." Lucan declared.

"Leviathan thinks the upcoming war is going to be won by having the most powerful players on his side. You, John, others. Truth is the board has

been set out and played already."

"What are you talking about?" Brite Bomber asked.

Lucan began to monologue,

"Raven, Reaper, and Ragnarok. These three are

operating in the shadows, underground, anywhere

they can't be seen. Plotting, scheming, thinking

about the next ten steps. I thought I was a knight,

powerful and mighty, but no. I am merely a pawn,

tormented at the pleasure of The Reaper. Raven

has betrayed me. And Ragnarok, I have my doubts

I am favorable by him."

"Leviathan is the king of this world, but not for longer. He has been getting weaker by the day, and his lackies, Fate and John, are not strong enough to defend this world. I mentioned three big bads, but I have a strong feeling more factions are developing as well."

"The own faction I was developing was annihilated by The Reaper, leaving only Blue Squire and Royale Knight on my team. And they were killed by him too. The Reaper... he even corrupted my wife. He took everything from me."

"This cell... it is not locked. I was allowed to escape whenever I was ready. But I am unsure I ever will be..."

"Take my Axecalibur. It does little against The Reaper, but you may find it useful in your journey. I will not need it, not now. I need to stay here in this cell and think. Brite Bomber, think about what I said. Go with John. I know he is pure."

Brite Bomber was still unsure of what to think but ended up taking Lucan's Axecalibur anyways. She left John and Lucan inside the cell and ran off.

While outside the prison, something began to happen to Brite Bomber. She felt a surge of energy coursing through her body, that made her uneasy. She began to get anxiety, and it worsened as the energy rippled throughout her body. She thought that her body was going to implode and gave an intense screech as the feeling turned unbearable.

"Brite Bomber!" John yelled out. "I'm coming!"

John escaped his cell, which was still unlocked, and ran as fast as he could to save Brite Bomber. Outside, he saw the backside of what appeared to be Brite Bomber looking over... another Brite Bomber.

What... is going on?

In an instant, the girl that appeared to be Brite Bomber picked up the fallen Brite Bomber's suppressed SMG and began to fire at John.

John, thanks to his training, immediately reacted, placing a wall in front of him, and proceeded to gain higher ground on his opponent.

Gotta gain the high ground on her, like Obi-Wan against Anakin. There! I've got a few stories on her. This suppressed pistol isn't ideal from this range, but it'll have to do.

John, in his attempt to quickly gain high ground on his opponent, did not notice that his enemy was weakening the base of his tower.

What? I'm falling down! No!

John fell from his tower but did not die thanks to only having built up five stories high. Once he fell, he immediately began to build again, this time, only to a third story. Once three-stories high, he peaked from his tower, and was shocked at what he saw.

No... this... Dark Bomber, she's got her hostage!

The Dark Bomber was holding Brite Bomber with

a suppressed SMG to her head. John was unsure of

what to do. He knew that she would not actually

die if the Dark Bomber killed her, after all, in The

Fortnite Source, people have multiple lives. But...

were Brite Bomber to die, Leviathan's strongest

ally would be weakened, leaving only John to carry

the weight of the team.

CRACK

The Dark Bomber dropped to the floor. A

mysterious man had shot her right in the head

with a sniper rifle. John looked towards the

direction of the gunshot and saw that a man in a

black and gold robe, with a cat mask, was building

towards Dark Bomber's direction.

This guy... his shot was dead-on, and he's building

so quickly...

The Dark Bomber, now angry, began to build

herself, going in the direction of the mysterious

man. In only a few seconds, their structures met,

beginning an epic build battle. They were evenly

matched, continuously meeting at the same story,

and neither could get a shot in.

The mysterious man, realizing that the build

battle would go on forever if he kept trying to gain

higher ground, decided to change his strategy in mid battle. He exited from his side of the now-massive structure and placed down a launch pad.

He then launch padded to John's tower, and immediately began to throw grenades at the base of the structure.

However, The Dark Bomber was not going to be taken down so easy, especially not by a tactic that she had used just minutes earlier against John. As the mysterious man was throwing grenades at the base of the structure, Dark Bomber was making her way towards the launch pad.

She ended up launch padding to an open hill directly in front of where the mysterious man and John were and began to do the double stairs double wall combination towards them.

This time, the mysterious man did not try to engage in a build battle against The Dark Bomber, and instead pulled out a tactical SMG from his robe and began to rip through her walls.

"You!" the mysterious man shouted at John. "Get down, and fire at her floors from below!"

John was scared. He came down from his structure when the mysterious man told him to, but in his panic, began to struggle to reload his suppressed pistol.

My hands... they're trembling too much!

Determining that she was in a bad position, The Dark Bomber began to fall back, and escaped the battle.

The mysterious man, seeing that The Dark Bomber fled, came down from John's structure, and dashed towards Brite Bomber, who was losing health and close to dying.

He began to heal her using a med kit, and gave her two minis to drink, preparing her in case they were to get attacked again.

"You feel better now?" the mysterious man asked.

Brite Bomber, still lying down on the ground, looked up to the mysterious man and said, "You... saved me."

Meanwhile, a disgruntled John looked away, feeling guilty that he could not save Brite Bomber.

I didn't do anything... This guy had to come outta nowhere to save her... I'm just like Lucan now... broken. I knew I wasn't meant for this... I don't know why I let Fate and Omen recruit me... I let Omen die... and Brite Bomber almost died because of me...

John made one step in the opposite direction of the mysterious man, and then another, and another... until John was nowhere to be found.

"John! John!" Brite Bomber shouted. "Where are you!?"

"Let him be. I know why he left. He left because he could not save you. He will be back." the mysterious man said.

"I hope you're right... you never told me your name." Brite Bomber said.

The mysterious man replied, "Drift."

Drift went on to tell Brite Bomber who he was and what his purpose was. Drift told Brite Bomber that he has one of the Hidden Keys, in fact, one of the most powerful Hidden Keys, The Rift Edge, which can pierce the dimensional plane.

He then told Brite Bomber many things about The

Hidden Keys that very few people knew about. He

had these things to say:

"These select pickaxes are named The Hidden

Keys because they each have a distinct hidden

ability, which can essentially 'unlock' something."

"For example, my Hidden Key, The Rift Edge,

unlocks the barrier that prevents interdimensional

travel. With the proper swing of The Rift Edge, I

can create a rift and use it to travel. However, I

have not mastered it yet. The Rift Edge belongs to

a class of Hidden Keys called The Bridge Keys."

"The Black Knight's Hidden Key, Axecalibur, is a Hidden Key that belongs to The Power Keys. Someone that masters that Hidden Key is a serious threat, for it can slice anything, and I mean anything, in half, and bypasses the amount of extra lives someone has in this world. You don't come back from the right swing of that Hidden Key."

"I do not know how many classes of Hidden Keys there are, nor where they all are, or who has which key. Me and my squad have been trying to capture all of them, to prevent them from getting into the wrong hands."

After Drift was finished talking about The Hidden Keys, Brite Bomber told him of Leviathan and Fate, and told Drift that he and his squad mates should join their efforts.

Drift was convinced, and they headed towards Lonely Lodge, where Leviathan would be with Fate, who had returned from her mission.

Chapter 5: Burn It Down

Looking towards the floor, Brite Bomber began to apologize to everyone inside the large cabin at Lonely Lodge,

"I'm so sorry... about everything..."

Leviathan looked at her and responded,

"You were manipulated. But even in your manipulation, you had only pure intentions. You had the genuine belief that we were evil, and so you were acting with benevolence."

Everyone began to circle around Brite Bomber and consoled her. They all told her that she should not let it get to her head, and to move forward. Many challenges were to come, and she was going to be needed for them.

Brite Bomber began to feel better, but still had a tremendous weight to carry on her, so she went upstairs and stayed in one of the rooms.

After Brite Bomber left, Leviathan was informed of everything that happened at the prison and gained new knowledge about The Hidden Keys.

Leviathan was surprised at the revelation that Lucan was now a broken soul, but not surprised at the fact that John had left. He understood the weight that John had to carry with him, having felt that he failed Omen in the past, and now Brite Bomber.

Leviathan was in accordance with Drift, who did not try to get John back. John was in a state of mind that he needed to change on his own. Nobody else was going to be able to make John better.

One thing that Leviathan was unsure what to think of, was the appearance of Dark Bomber. Was it The Raven's doing? Perhaps, but he thought it was best to not jump to conclusions.

What he was most surprised with was the existence of Drift. First, he was surprised that he never knew about Drift, and second, his Hidden Key changed everything that Leviathan had prophesized.

You see, Leviathan had thought John was going to be the bridge between worlds, thanks to his potential of unlocking Love Wings, but Drift's Hidden Key, Rift Edge, has that ability too. So then, what is the purpose of John? Was recruiting John a mistake? Is that why John disappeared – because he simply is not fit to be a savior of worlds?

But Leviathan did not want to give up on John. John had a greater purpose, he was sure of it. Just, nobody knew what that purpose was, not yet.

After getting informed with new and valuable knowledge, Leviathan reciprocated, telling the team about Fate's mission.

"Fate went on a mission to repair her Oracle Axe, which was damaged in a fight long ago. Fate, Omen, and I always knew of the Oracle Axe's powers, but with this new knowledge of the existence of the Hidden Keys, I feel that there are properties of the Oracle Axe that have not been discovered yet."

"She went to Ragnarok to have it fixed. I realize now that Ragnarok may in fact be our enemy, but I cannot make such an accusation based on what Lucan, The Black Knight, has stated. For hundreds of thousands of years, Ragnarok has been the repairman of this world, helping to repair not only physical items, but holes within our world. He has been invaluable."

"Once Fate had her Oracle Axe fixed, she was instructed to use it to find others like John, like Brite Bomber, because we will need as many allies as possible in the upcoming battles. She identified several people that will be of great use to us in the future."

Leviathan had more to say but was interrupted by a worried Fate.

"Leviathan, I sense someone coming..."

Outside, a man yelled, "Launch your grenades!"

Dozens and dozens of grenades could be seen outside curving through the air, cooked, so that they would explode before coming into contact with the ground.

BOOM! BOOM!

BOOM! BOOM!

Multiple explosions went off mid-air, acting as a warning of sorts.

Everyone inside Lonely Lodge – Leviathan, Fate, Brite Bomber, and Drift, scurried outside, escaping from the back of the large cabin, and ran towards the direction of the ocean.

Drift, acting out of bravery, built up a staircase to see what was going on, and saw dozens of what appeared to be steel soldiers, with a man in a black body suit commanding them. Drift was spotted.

The man in the black body suit pointed at Drift and asked, "You there, Cat's Mask, where is Leviathan?"

"No need to waste my explosives when he can give us what we want."

Drift replied, "We won't give you anything!"

Drift, let's go! Leviathan telepathically told Drift.

Near the ocean, Brite Bomber told Leviathan that they couldn't just leave Lonely Lodge defenseless. She told him that if they were going to run away, then so be it, but she had to atone for her betrayal, and she was going to fight.

Leviathan stood his ground, stating that they were at a disadvantage, numerically and environmentally, they only had a small team and were on the low ground. It could only end in death for them. But Brite Bomber didn't care and pushed forward.

Brite Bomber was prepared the entire time. The moment she heard explosions, she knew there was trouble, and took great amounts of resources, and a gun, from the Lonely Lodge stockpile.

She began to make her way towards the hills in front of Lonely Lodge, building double stairs and double walls to do so.

The man in the black body suit spotted her and ordered his men to pull out their guns and fire at her. As each soldier began to pull out their LMGs, Drift began to rush them as well, but this time from the opposite side that Brite Bomber was rushing.

Drift pulled out his double hand cannons and began popping off shots at the head of the steel soldiers. Two by two, they began to fall, but there were so many of them, that Drift felt like he was accomplishing nothing.

There's so many of them... and... what?

To his surprise, the steel soldiers began to get back up, as if they had no limit to their health.

With the steel soldier's focus diverted from her, Brite Bomber began to circle around Lonely Lodge and try to get a sneak attack on the man in the black body suit, from his side.

He's commanding his units to change their tactics against Drift... this is my chance to make up for what I did! In my hurry, I could only get this burst-assault rifle, but it's perfect in this situation... now... gotta line this up perfectly... ready... aim... and f –

In a split-second, the man in the black body suit pulled out two compact SMGs and mowed down Brite Bomber. She was on the ground, severely damaged, needing a revival.

"BRITE!" Drift screamed. *I can't do anything to help her! She's all the way over there! I... have to try this.*

Before drift attempted to slice at the sky with his Drift Edge, hopelessly attempting to somehow transport himself to Brite Bomber's location, large gunshots began to be heard from behind the man in the black body suit and his soldiers.

The man in the black body suit turned away from executing Brite Bomber, and looked face-to-face with another man in black, The Black Knight.

The Black Knight fired a shot into the man in the black body suit and knocked him down.

Meanwhile, Drift found himself in an unusual place.

What is this, where am I? I'm in a room, and it's all red...

Who is that in the corner?

"I'm Omen." the man said.

"Omen?" a confused Drift asked.

"Fate's brother." Omen said.

"Oh." Drift sighed.

"I don't know what this place is either." Omen said.

"It feels like I've been stuck here for an eternity, trying to get out. I hear owls coming from places where there is no space and should be no sound."

"Sometimes, a little television appears inside this room, and all it plays are war-movies, in black and white. Drift, is there war going on outside?"

Drift replied with,

"There is a battle at Lonely Lodge going on, but not a war."

"Drift..." Omen dragged out.

"... the true enemy of the world is not inside, but outside. He has not yet revealed himself and will not reveal himself until he is here. He is coming soon. Leviathan is weak, Fate is not a soldier, Brite Bomber is too kind, and John – he is not a leader. The rest of your comrades, they are too green."

"Drift, you – "

The world began to shake and crumble. Omen realized this, and yelled out one final thing to Drift,

"Six Sacred Squads!"

Once the world crumbled, Drift found himself back in the Fortnite Source. However, he was not back at Lonely Lodge. He was sitting in a chair, directly in front of The Raven.

Back at Lonely Lodge, the battle continued. Right when the man in the black body suit fell, The Black Knight began to build himself a concrete tower and rained down fire on the steel soldiers who began to target him with his modified revolver.

His modified revolver was so powerful that it was destroying the steel soldiers each in one hit.

The man in the black body suit healed himself while on the floor and began to fire at the base of The Black Knight's tower, destroying it quickly, thanks to the fire-rate of the dual compact SMGs.

Anticipating that move, The Black Knight leaped towards the man in the black body suit and took him down to the ground. Now positioned directly on top of him, The Black Knight aimed right at his face and fired, but the man was able to dodge by moving his head. Immediately after, a power struggle ensued, as the man attempted to grab The Black Knight's gun.

During the power struggle, some of the steel

soldiers began to intervene, shooting directly at

The Black Knight, causing him to react and build

around himself, and his enemy.

As The Black Knight was building, the man in the

black body suit grabbed his leg and dropped him to

the floor.

The tides soon began to change as Leviathan and

Fate finally arrived at the battle, late, but who had

gone back to the cabin to get greater firepower.

Armed with RPGs, they began to destroy the steel

soldiers with ease.

Hearing the explosions, and understanding that the tides were turned, the man in the black body suit gave an order: burn all the buildings!

Without hesitation, the steel soldiers obeyed the order. One by one, they ran like wild animals towards all the key structures in Lonely Lodge and began to self-destruct.

BOOM! BOOM!

BOOM! BOOM!

The Black Knight got up and tried to finish off the man in the black body suit once and for all but saw that he was gone.

Trees began to catch on fire, and soon, all Lonely Lodge was burning. Temperatures rose, and the heat began to become dangerously high. Leviathan started to become incredibly weak.

Drift, who mysteriously returned from being face-to-face with The Raven, went to go pick up Brite Bomber, and then located Leviathan and Fate.

The fires were ravaging throughout the area, consuming everything in its path.

There was only one thing that Drift could do that would ensure that they would escape the area, and that was to use his Drift Edge to tear open a rift in the sky and take everyone with him.

Putting Brite Bomber down on the ground, he pulled out his Drift Edge and sliced at the sky. Nothing happened. He tried again. Nothing happened. Frustrated, he began to swing violently at the sky, and hoped that *something* would happen. But nothing did.

Knowing that everyone would die if he did not do something, Leviathan pulled from the little life energy he had and did the astonishing.

The ocean behind Lonely Lodge began to rise, high enough until it began to flood the entire area. Leviathan, acting on only instinct, could not compose himself to control the water, causing the waves to become very violent.

"The waves are going to smash us against the mountain in front of us!" Drift shouted.

Leviathan's attempt at extinguishing the fires and saving everyone resulted in a greater danger that could drown everyone in the Fortnite Source. As the danger loomed closer, Drift held Fate's hand, and awaited the waves to come and either smash them into a wall or drown them.

People have multiple lives in the Fortnite Source,

but they knew that once the world would be

completely submerged in water, the little extra

lives they had would be meaningless as they would

have to respawn and immediately begin to drown.

But Leviathan began to drift into the sky, in an

angelic fashion. He was glowing, and he had his

hands held out.

"Stop."

All the water that was on land vanished.

Everything went back to normal.

Descending down, Leviathan began to heal Brite Bomber, bringing her back to full strength. Once Brite Bomber was brought back to full strength, Leviathan materialized a small, colorful, and translucent notebook that had a divine aura to it and gave it to fate.

Softly and with sorrow, Leviathan began to give his final worlds,

"My time is over. In that notebook, is everything you need to know about the Fortnite Source. Take care of this world as I have taken care of it, and you. I will no longer exist, but a part of me will always be here. Thank you all for easing my loneliness..."

Leviathan began to slowly disappear.

Fate began to cry and yelled,

"Leviathan! No!"

Brite Bomber, tears held back, and fists clenched, began to mutter,

"No... "

The Fortnite Source was saved, but at the cost of Leviathan. Fate, Brite Bomber, and Drift now have to continue without their beloved wise leader guiding them. Rest in peace, Leviathan.

Chapter 6: Permanent Changes

A week after the destruction of Lonely Lodge, Fate, Brite Bomber, and Drift found themselves at a large mansion, which they found after following a map inside the notebook that Leviathan gave them.

There, they were instructed to make the mansion the new base of operations. Everything inside the mansion was hi-tech, and easy to use. It was a much better headquarters than Lonely Lodge.

The day they arrived at the mansion, Brite Bomber mentioned that she had been in it before, claiming that she was pulled out of a game of Fortnite and taken to the mansion by The Reaper.

Fate said that that was impossible, considering that The Spectral Notebook said that this mansion is a contingency plan in the event of Leviathan's death. A part of his power was placed on top of this land a long time ago to react to his potential death and transform into the mansion.

Fate continued, stating that nobody could have possibly even known what the mansion was going to look like. And even if they did know what the mansion was going to look like, and could create an illusion of it – what purpose would that serve?

Brite Bomber nodded and told Fate that she might have just been having false memories.

The mansion was filled with chests that were packed with weapons, explosives, healing items, and resources, and there was a complex security room too. Not to mention, food was abundant, but it was mostly weird recipes mixing apples and mushrooms. Yuck! Probably super healthy though.

The rest of the first day at the mansion was spent mourning and sleeping. Fate, Brite Bomber, and Drift went through a lot of stress, and were exhausted from the journey to find the mansion.

During the second day at the mansion, they began

to plan for the future.

"What do we do about John?" Brite Bomber asked.

Drift responded,

"I will go search for him myself, after deciding on a

likely location that he is in."

Fate began to talk,

"At Lonely Lodge, we were severely outnumbered,

and outgunned. We might have even been out

skilled. For whatever reason, The Black Knight

arrived and tremendously upped our odds at survival that day. Had he not arrived…"

"… we might have all gotten killed before Leviathan saved us. I am confident that both of you would have respawned, but… with how weakened I am now, I do not think that would have been the case for me."

"You know, there is something I find funny. You mentioned John and this thought came up. When I was training John, I tried to play the happy-go-lucky girl. I thought that maybe it would help with my mourning over my brother Omen. And now, this all happens. The death of Leviathan. A father figure to me. And now I know that smiling is irrelevant, for the world finds ways to invert it."

"Even with this mansion, I am unsure that we will be able to save the world."

Brite Bomber became angry, slapped Fate across the face, and yelled,

"What the heck is wrong with you!?"

"Unsure that we will be able to save the world? So, what, you want us to give up? Just give up? Let The Reaper and the man that attacked us at Lonely do whatever they want? Is that what you want? Then we don't need you, coward!"

Drift attempted to calm down Brite Bomber, grabbing her by the shoulder and saying,

"Hey... hey, Brite – she's just traumatized. Let her vent."

Brite Bomber pushed Drift's hand away and yelled,

"No! I'm not going to let her vent. Because she's going to start believing all that negative stuff in her head and then we're going to lose her."

"You keep telling yourself that everything is pointless, and it becomes pointless because you made it that way. And then you can't crawl out of that hole."

Fate interrupted in a gloomy manner,

"It is pointless. I am being pragmatic. We might as well just enjoy the comfort of this mansion for how little it lasts. I am weak, and so are you. I remember you distinctly having to be saved by Drift."

Brite Bomber was now furious,

"I was trying to take down the enemy while you were hiding! What the heck did you do, miss princess!?"

Fate, becoming heated herself, responded,

"... Leviathan... and I did more than you did. We destroyed many of the enemy soldiers. You just let yourself get severely wounded."

Drift tried to calm down the situation, to no avail.

Fed up with Fate's mouth, Brite Bomber charged at her, and knocked her down to the ground. There, she began to beat on Fate. Fate just let herself get hit, before Drift stepped in and tossed Brite Bomber away.

Fate began to cry, but not because of Brite Bomber hitting her, but because she was upset with herself.

"I'm... so weak... I'm helpless... Leviathan, I don't know what to do without him..."

"... I've always been this way... I got caught by the enemy before you two were even here, and John and Omen tried to rescue me... and I got killed that day..."

"... I got killed but I was able to come back because I still had an extra life left... but Omen died that day, for me, to save me... because he believed that I was worth saving. But what have I done since then? Nothing! ... nothing!"

Fate's cries became heavier, and she began to shout,

"... I am worthless! Leviathan has joined Omen... in the fruitless sacrifice of saving me...!"

Drift and Brite Bomber just looked at Fate, unsure of what to do with her. Brite Bomber began to feel empathy for Fate, as she too had a great weight to carry, the weight of betrayal.

Eventually, Fate stopped crying, and was consoled by both Drift and Brite. Drift was just glad that the two girls, the only girls, in the group stopped fighting. He had absolutely no clue as to what to do in that situation.

The next few days were filled with awkward silence, as each member had their own demons to battle with, and energy to recover.

A week and a half into being in the mansion, Drift brought Brite Bomber and Fate together, and told them about a discovery he made. The Spectral Notebook revealed several new pages inside of it.

When Leviathan originally gave The Spectral Notebook to Fate, it only had a map inside of it. But now, there was much more on it. It seemed to have grown, like an organic, living, object.

They went to the mansion's command center and

began to read The Spectral Notebook together.

My passing has brought about great change in this

world. This world is a living world, that even though was

made by me, is not entirely controlled by me. While I

do not entirely control this world, I do have one

important role in it: maintaining the life force of the

inhabitants here.

To put it simply, every time someone in this world has

died, my life was automatically given to them to bring

them back. I did not want to tell you, Fate, this, as I

know how your response would have been to that declaration. Omen never knew either.

That is one of the reasons why I have become weak over my very long life, because I have been constantly giving a part of me away to others. My perpetual loneliness has made me want to sustain the life of the spirits I created long ago.

Now with my passing, a great change has occurred.

NOBODY HAS MORE THAN ONE LIFE IN THE FORTNITE SOURCE ANYMORE.

Death is permanent. There is no coming back in a weakened state, like previously. It is simply a new rule in The Fortnite Source. As time passes, and powerful players inside our world continue to tamper with the environment, more changes may take place to how we live in the Fortnite Source. The essence of combat may even change.

My death also means that the world is less stable. Changes to the physical environment may occur. New areas may rise and disappear in an arbitrary fashion. Time will become fluid.

For now, you must all recruit as many members to join your efforts and find the Hidden Keys. The mansion has everything you need to succeed. Take care of this book. New knowledge will be displayed as needed and disappear soon after to prevent enemies from taking it.

The final page ended with:

THE RACE TO FIND THE HIDDEN KEYS HAS BEGUN. GOOD LUCK.

Epilogue

A SPACESHIP IS DRIFTING IN THE

VOID OF SPACE, QUITE A DISTANCE

AWAY FROM THE FORTNITE SOURCE.

IN IT, ARE WHAT APPEAR TO BE

ASTRONAUTS. THEY ARE HUMAN-LIKE.

INSIDE THE SPACESHIP, A DISCUSSION

IS TAKING PLACE.

"Jumping from planet to planet without any

resistance has been boring, don't you agree?"

"I agree sir. It appears that the mere sighting of our spaceship alone causes people to give up resistance. These low-level beings shatter themselves at the thought of an advanced people like us coming."

"How about we do something different. Instead of going planet after planet, how about we try crossing over into worlds inside other dimensions?"

"Sir, that technology has been lost to us…"

"…during our battle with The Ravens, they destroyed The Librarian, our great spaceship containing a myriad of knowledge."

"Do you think I do not remember that? How the stolen knowledge of countless planets, that I was responsible for obtaining, was completely destroyed by my brother informing The Ravens of our location, and our weaknesses? They knew the meeting that was taking place in that ship, killing off many Leviathans that were in attendance. Now, all that is left is this ship and a skeleton crew in a universe foreign to us, as we were displaced by The Ravens."

"What I need you to do, along with Mission Specialist, is recreate that technology. We have been trying to forget about that incident for so long that it almost quenched our desire for revenge. But alas, it is a feeling that will never subside. My

brother, and The Ravens, must be exterminated..."

"There is a planet, sir, that we have detected

with great technology. Planet Roblox. We

believe that the technology in this world can

be reengineered into something akin to what

we had previously. However, there is

something unusual about that planet, sir."

"First, we have detected high levels of

toxicity, unusually high. Now the real

strange thing is that we have detected people

from a different dimension that have crossed

over into this world as well..."

"... potential competition for us, if and when we arrive there. Due to the toxicity of the planet, and potential warzone that it will become, I suggest we send Toxic Trooper and Hazard Agent to investigate."

"I concur with that idea. Set course to that planet immediately. Once we steal their technology, let's visit The Fortnite Source and see how my brother, Leviathan is doing. I fully expect him to be a serious threat by now, after all, he is the reincarnation of The First Leviathan."

Continue The Story Yourself!

Other Books You'll Love

Follow Brite Bomber on her road to stardom!

If you still haven't read it, make sure to pick up a copy of Brite Bomber's Victory Royale! It's the book that set up the entire Fortnite Tale series.

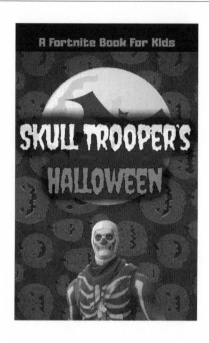

Action-packed and filled with scares and twists. Includes

pictures!

Skull Trooper's Halloween is also connected to the Fortnite Tale

series – taking place after this book! It's an awesome book that

can be read at any time, not just Halloween.

Worlds will collide in this EPIC crossover! Over 30 pictures!

This is an amazing book that I had a lot of fun writing. It's packed with action, adventure, and world building. You don't have to have any experience with Roblox and Minecraft to enjoy it either.

Based on this book's Epilogue, it seems that Roblox Meets Minecraft and Fortnite Tale are closely connected...

Outside of the books mentioned, I have a lot of original series

that will be released in the future!

To keep up with me on everything I have planned, check out my

social media! Info on the next two pages.

Social Media

I have the following:

1. Amazon Author Page

2. Goodreads Author Profile

3. Instagram Profile

4. Facebook Page

You can follow me on whichever platform you prefer, but for parents, it is easiest to **leave me a follow-on Amazon.** By following me on Amazon, you get e-mailed right away when I release my next book.

 You can also message me on any of those platforms and I'll reply as quickly as I can! Usually, within the same day! I love talking to my fans – sometimes I even take fan ideas and put them into my books! I added Drift into this book because of a fan idea!

instagram.com/authorartbooks | #authorart #authorartbooks

facebook.com/authorartbooks

goodreads.com/authorart

authorart@authorartbooks.com

My website is coming soon too – which I'm designing myself!

www.authorartbooks.com

Glossary

Words are listed in order of appearance and defined as how they are used in the context of the story.

The most challenging words to pronounce are given their pronunciation.

Hints about the next book may be in the sentence examples!

Semantics - The meaning of a word, phrase, sentence, or text.

How It's Pronounced: Si(ck) – man – ticks

My English teacher gave me a C on my paper because of my misuse of semantics.

Facade – An appearance used by someone to hide something about themselves.

This word is weird. When you see it, you think it's pronounced Fake-Aid, but, nope! This is because it comes from the French word façade.

How It's Pronounced: Fuh – Sawed

Has Leviathan been using a Facade all this time?

Copyright Infringement – Using someone else's work without their permission.

My friend got in trouble for copyright infringement when he used characters from Marvel in his script for a movie without their permission.

Lament – An expression of sadness.

How It's Pronounced: Luh – Meant

Did you lament when Leviathan died?

Interject – An interruption.

I like to interject in my friend's conversations when I feel like I have something to add to them.

Belittle – To make someone feel like less of themselves.

The Raven thinks he's all that, always trying to belittle others.

Dwindle – To grow less in size or number.
My mom's money began to dwindle when I started buying v-bucks every day.

Increment – An increase of something.

I think Fortnite's player base grows at an increment of ten thousand players a day.

Incognito – Having your identity concealed.

How It's Pronounced: In – Cawg – Nee – Toe

Are there people in Fortnite Tale that are incognito that we don't know about yet?

Subtle – Something that is not so obvious.

How It's Pronounced: Suh – Toll

To find the Hidden Keys, Drift and his team must be subtle.

Trivial – Not important.

How It's Pronounced: Trih – Vee – Uhl

It may seem trivial at first to learn how to build properly, but it's important down the road.

Prophesize – To make a prediction.

<u>How It's Pronounced</u>: Prawf - Uh – Size

I wonder who can prophesize better, Fate or Raven.

Deity – A god or goddess.

<u>How It's Pronounced</u>: Dee – Uh – Tee

Is it possible that Leviathan is a deity?

Liaison – The link between something.

<u>How It's Pronounced</u>: Lee – Ay – Zon

Is it possible that Leviathan is a deity?

Cosmic – Relating to the universe.

Fortnite Tale may be a story set in a larger cosmic scale, outside of just Earth and the Fortnite Source.

Nuisance – Something or someone that is an annoyance.

How It's Pronounced: Nooh – Sunss

The Reaper is a big nuisance that must be dealt.

Confidant – A person whom you trust with important information and secrets.

I wonder what information the Blue Squire and Royale Knight had about The Black Knight.

Concussive – Force relating to the impact on someone's head.

How It's Pronounced: Cunn – Cuss – Ivv

Did Lucan suffer from brain damage because of the concussive force that he took from The Reaper using Axecalibur?

Consciousness – Being awake and aware of your surroundings.

How It's Pronounced: Cawn – Shush – Ness

I think if I was in Fortnite Tale and saw Leviathan raising the ocean, I would lose consciousness.

Demoralize – To cause someone to lose their confidence.

The Raven and The Reaper are the type of people that will try to demoralize you at any chance they get.

Groggy – To feel weak and dazed.

I'm always groggy when I wake up.

Foresight – The ability to predict the future.

I wonder if it was really true that The Raven had better foresight than Leviathan.

Interdimensional – In between dimensions.

Will the astronauts be able to successfully invade Planet Roblox and then interdimensional travel to the Fortnite Source?

Manipulate – To try to influence someone.

The Raven likes to Manipulate people.

Benevolence – Being kind and pure.

How It's Pronounced: Buh – Neh – Vuh – Lenss

Because of Leviathan's benevolence, the Fortnite Source was saved… for the time being.

Accordance – To be in agreement with.

Me and my best friend are always in accordance with each other.

Reciprocate – To give in return.

<u>How It's Pronounced</u>: Rih – Sip – Ruh – Kate

I try to reciprocate all the love my parents give me.

Accusation – Claiming that someone has done something.

<u>How It's Pronounced</u>: Ack – You – Zay - Shun

Someone made the accusation that I cheated on my homework, but I did not.

Intervene – To step in.

Brite Bomber is the type of girl that will intervene when the situation calls for it, but it might cost her in the future.

Angelic – Like an angel.

How It's Pronounced: Ann – Jel - Ick

My mom told me that when I dance, I come off as angelic, but I think I come off as weird.

Materialize – To create something out of nothing.

How It's Pronounced: Muh – Tear – Eeh – Uh - Lies

I wish I had the power to materialize things, I would make a lot of prepaid cards to buy V-Bucks with!

Translucent – Semi-transparent.

How It's Pronounced: Trans – Lou – Scent

I saw a video of some weird sea creature that is translucent, you can kind of see through it!

Clench – To close tightly.

I always clench my hands when I'm angry.

Happy-Go-Lucky – Cheerful and carefree.

I'm always happy-go-lucky when I'm allowed to play Fortnite.

Invert – To put something in the opposite way.

I wonder how well I would do in Fortnite in a controller invert challenge.

Gloomy – Sad.

The Fortnite Source has become gloomy without Leviathan, but things may get even worse now that there's less leadership.

Pragmatic – Practical.

Unless you're an experienced pro, it's better that you play pragmatic than flashy in Fortnite.

Perpetual – Never ending or changing.

How It's Pronounced: Purr – Petch – You – Uhl

Fortnite would be boring if it was perpetual.

Arbitrary – Something random.

How It's Pronounced: Arr – Bih – Trar - Ee

I made the arbitrary choice that today I was going to only land at Lazy Links.

Quench – Satisfy thirst.

There is nothing that can quench me better after practice than a cold bottle of water.

Myriad – Countless.

How It's Pronounced: Mirr(or) – Ee – Ad

I wish I had a myriad of v-bucks!

Subside – Become less intense.

I don't think the violence in the Fortnite Source will subside, I think it'll grow and then turn into a great war.

34113102R00123

Made in the USA
Middletown, DE
22 January 2019